Marx Joyce Abbott Hardy Montaigne Machiavelli Chesterton Cooper Emerson Austen Defoe Melville Haggard Hugo Eliot Grimm Christie Carroll Stoker Molière Wilde Maupassant Byron Schiller Engels Garnett Einstein Fitzgerald Hawthorne Smith Kafka Goethe Dostoyevsky Cotton Hall Baum Kipling Doyle Willis Leslie Dumas Henry Nietzsche Flaubert Turgenev Balzac Stockton Vatsyayana Crane Burroughs Verne Whitman Gogol Curtis Tocqueville Vinci Homer Widger Tolstoy Busch Darwin Thoreau Scott Potter Freud Zola Twain Plato Lawrence Kant Jowett Stevenson Dickens Andersen Cervantes Burton Hesse Harte London Descartes Voltaire Poe Aristotle Wells Hale James Hastings Cooke Bunner Shakespeare Richter Chambers Irving da Doré Chekhov Shaw Benedict Alcott Swift Dante Wodehouse Pushkin Newton tredition®

tredition was established in 2006 by Sandra Latusseck and Soenke Schulz. Based in Hamburg, Germany, tredition offers publishing solutions to authors and publishing houses, combined with worldwide distribution of printed and digital book content. tredition is uniquely positioned to enable authors and publishing houses to create books on their own terms and without conventional manufacturing risks.

For more information please visit: www.tredition.com

TREDITION CLASSICS

This book is part of the TREDITION CLASSICS series. The creators of this series are united by passion for literature and driven by the intention of making all public domain books available in printed format again - worldwide. Most TREDITION CLASSICS titles have been out of print and off the bookstore shelves for decades. At tredition we believe that a great book never goes out of style and that its value is eternal. Several mostly non-profit literature projects provide content to tredition. To support their good work, tredition donates a portion of the proceeds from each sold copy. As a reader of a TREDITION CLASSICS book, you support our mission to save many of the amazing works of world literature from oblivion. See all available books at www.tredition.com.

Project Gutenberg

The content for this book has been graciously provided by Project Gutenberg. Project Gutenberg is a non-profit organization founded by Michael Hart in 1971 at the University of Illinois. The mission of Project Gutenberg is simple: To encourage the creation and distribution of eBooks. Project Gutenberg is the first and largest collection of public domain eBooks.

Zoe

Evelyn Whitaker

Imprint

This book is part of TREDITION CLASSICS

Author: Evelyn Whitaker
Cover design: Buchgut, Berlin – Germany

Publisher: tredition GmbH, Hamburg - Germany
ISBN: 978-3-8472-1317-8

www.tredition.com
www.tredition.de

The intention of the TREDITION CLASSICS series is to make world literature in the public domain available in printed format. Literary enthusiasts and organizations, such as Project Gutenberg, worldwide have scanned and digitally edited the original texts. tredition has subsequently formatted and redesigned the content into a modern reading layout. Therefore, we cannot guarantee the exact reproduction of the original format of a particular historic edition. Please also note that no modifications have been made to the spelling, therefore it may differ from the orthography used today.

ZOE
BY THE AUTHOR OF "LADDIE," "TIP-CAT," &c.

ZOE

BY THE AUTHOR OF

'LADDIE,' 'DON,' 'POMONA,' 'BELLE,' 'PHOEBE'S HERO,'
'MISS TOOSEY'S MISSION,' 'TIP CAT,' ETC.

LONDON: 38 Soho Square. W.1
W. & R. CHAMBERS, LIMITED
EDINBURGH: 339 High Street

1890

CONTENTS

ZOE.

CHAPTER I.

The Christening—An Outlandish Name—The Organist's Mistake—Farm-work—Tom and Bill—The Baby—Baby and All

Hath this child been already baptised, or no?'

'No, she ain't; leastwise we don't know as how she 've been or no, so we thought as we 'd best have her done.'

The clergyman who was taking Mr Clifford's duty at Downside for that Sunday, thought that this might be the usual undecided way of answering among the natives, and proceeded with the service. There were two other babies also brought that afternoon, one of which was crying lustily, so that it was not easy to hear what the sponsors answered; and, moreover, the officiating clergyman was a young man, and the prospect of holding that screaming, red-faced, little object made him too nervous and anxious to get done with it to stop and make further inquiries.

The woman who returned this undecided answer was an elderly woman, with a kind, sunburnt, honest face, very much heated just now, and embarrassed too; for the baby in her arms prevented her getting at her pocket handkerchief to wipe the perspiration from her brow and pulling her bonnet on to its proper position on her head. The man beside her was also greatly embarrassed, and kept shuffling his large hob-nailed shoes together, and turning his hat round and round in his fingers.

I think that really that hat was the chief cause of his discomfort, for he was so accustomed to have it on his head that he could not feel quite himself without it; and, indeed, his wife could hardly recognise him, as she had been accustomed to see him wearing it indoors and out during the twenty years of their married life; pushed back for meals or smoking, but always on his head, except in bed, and even there, report says, on cold winter nights, he had recourse to it to keep off the draught from that cracked pane in the window. His face, like his wife's, was weatherbeaten, and of the same broad, flat type as hers, with small, surprised, dazzled-looking, pale blue eyes, and a tangle of grizzled light hair under his chin. He was noticeable for the green smock-frock he wore, a garment which is so rapidly disappearing before the march of civilisation, and giving place to the ill-cut, ill-made coat of shoddy cloth, which is fondly thought to resemble the squire's.

The christening party was completed by a hobbledehoy lad of about sixteen, who tried to cover his invincible shyness by a grin, and to keep his foolish eyes from the row of farm boys in the aisle, whose critical glances he felt in every pore. He was so like both father and mother, that there was no mistaking his parentage; but when Mrs Gray took off the shepherd's-plaid shawl in which the baby was wrapped, such a little dark head and swarthy face were exposed to view as might have made intelligent spectators (if there were any in Downside church that afternoon, which I doubt) reflect on the laws of heredity and reversion to original types.

'Name this child!'

The clergyman had got successfully through his business with the roaring George Augustus and the whimpering Alberta Florence, and had now the little, quiet, brown-faced baby in his arms. Even a young and unmarried man was fain to confess that it was an unusually pretty little face that lay against his surplice, with a pointed chin, and more eyebrows and lashes than most young babies possess, and with dark eyes that looked up at him with a certain intelligence, recognisable even to an unprejudiced observer.

'Name this child!'

Mrs Gray had taken advantage of this opportunity to mop her forehead with her blue and white pocket handkerchief, and wrestle with her bonnet's unconquerable tendency to slip off behind, and the clergyman passed the question on to her husband, who fixed his eye on a bluebottle buzzing in one of the windows, and jerked out what sounded like 'Joe.'

'I thought it was a girl,' whispered the clergyman. 'Joe, did you say?'

'No, it ain't that 'zactly. Here, 'Liza, can't you tell the gentleman? You knows best what it be.'

The next attempt sounded like 'Sue,' and the clergyman suggested Susan as the name, but that would not do.

'Zola' seemed to him, though not a reader of French novels, unsuitable, and 'Zero,' too, he could not quite appreciate.

'I can't make it out, an outlandish sorter name!' said Gray, with a terrible inclination to put on his hat in the excitement of the moment, only checked by a timely nudge from his wife's elbow; 'here, ain't you got it wrote down somewheres? Can't you show it up?'

And after a lengthened rummage in a voluminous pocket, and the production of several articles irrelevant to the occasion—a thimble, a bit of ginger, and part of a tract—Mrs Gray brought to light a piece of paper, on which was written the name 'Zoe.'

'Zoe, I baptise thee'——

A sudden crash on the organ-pedals followed these words. Mr Robins, the organist, had, perhaps, been asleep and let his foot slip on to the pedals, or, perhaps, he had thought there was no wind in the instrument and that he could put his foot down with impunity. He was plainly very much ashamed of himself for what had happened, and it was only right that he should be, for, of course, it made all the school children giggle, and a good many of their elders too, who should have known better.

The boy who blew the organ declared that he turned quite red and bent his head over the keys as if he were examining something on them, and he was evidently nervous and upset, for he made ever so many mistakes in the concluding parts of the service, and, to the great surprise and to the satisfaction of the blower, cut the voluntary at the end unusually short, ending it in an abrupt and discordant way, which, I am sorry to say, the blower described as 'a 'owl,' though any shock that the boy's musical taste sustained was compensated for by the feeling that he would be at home at least ten minutes earlier than usual to tea.

Now it so happened that Mr Robins was in the vestry when the christening party came in to give the particulars about the babies to be entered in the register. He had come to fetch a music-book, which, however, it appeared after all had been left at home; but the clergyman was glad of his help in making out the story of the little Zoe who had just been baptised.

I have spoken before of intelligent observers noticing and drawing arguments from the entire want of likeness between Zoe and her parents; but all the observers on this occasion whether intelligent or not, with the exception of the officiating clergyman, were quite aware that Zoe was not the Grays' baby, but was a foundling child picked up one night by Gray in his garden.

Of her antecedents nothing was known, and, of course, any sensible people would have sent her to the workhouse—every one agreed on this point and told the Grays so; and yet, I think, half the women who were so positive and severe on Mrs Gray's folly would have done just the same.

We do not half of us know how kind-hearted we are till we are tried, or perhaps it is our foolishness that we do not realise.

Gray was only a labourer with twelve shillings a week and a couple of pounds more at harvest; and, of course, in bad weather there was no work and no wages, which is the rule among the agricultural labourers about Downside, as in many other parts, so did not present itself as a grievance to Gray's mind, though, to be sure, in winter or wet seasons it was a hard matter to get along. But it was neighbours' fare, and none of them felt hardly used, for Farmer Benson, what with bad seasons and cattle plague, was not much better off than they were, and the men knew it.

But out of these wages it was hardly to be expected of the most provident of people that anything could be laid by for old age or a rainy day; indeed, there seemed so many rainy days in the present that it was not easy to give much thought to those in the future. Of course too the local provident club had come to utter and hopeless grief. Is there any country place where this has not been the case?

Gray had paid into it regularly for years and had gone every Whitmonday to its dinner, his one voluntary holiday during the year, on which occasion he took too much beer as a sort of solemn duty connected with his membership. When it collapsed he was too old to join another club, and so was left stranded. He bore it very philosophically; indeed, I think it was only on Whitmonday that he felt it at all, as it seemed strange and unnatural to go to bed quite sober on that day, as he did on all other days of the year.

On all other occasions he was a thoroughly sober man, perhaps, however, more from necessity than choice, as the beer supplied by Farmer Benson in the hayfield was of a quality on which, as the men said, you got 'no forrarder' if you drank a hogshead, and Gray had no money to spare from the necessaries of life to spend on luxury, even the luxury of getting drunk.

He was in one way better off than his neighbours from a worldly point of view, in that he had not a large family as most of them were blessed with; for children are a blessing, a gift and heritage that cometh of the Lord, even when they cluster round a cold hearth and a scanty board. But Gray had only two sons, the elder of whom, Tom, we have seen at Zoe's christening, and who had been at work four years, having managed at twelve to scramble into the fifth standard, and at once left school triumphantly, and now can neither read nor write, having clean forgotten everything drummed into his head, but earns three shillings and sixpence a week going along with Farmer Benson's horses, from five o'clock in the morning till six in the evening, the long wet furrows and heavy ploughed land having made havoc of his legs, as such work does with most plough-boys.

The younger boy, Bill, is six years younger and still at school, and having been a delicate child, or as his mother puts it, 'enjoying bad health,' is not promising for farm-work, and, being fond of his book and a favourite at school, his mother cherishes hopes of his becoming a school-teacher in days to come.

But such is the perversity of human nature, that though many a Downside mother with a family of little steps envied Mrs Gray her compact family and the small amount of washing attached to it, that ungrateful woman yearned after an occupant for the old wooden cradle, and treasured up the bits of baby things that had belonged to Tom and Bill, and nursed up any young thing that came to hand and wanted care, bringing up a motherless blind kitten with assiduous care and patience, as if the supply of that commodity was not always largely in excess of the demand, and lavishing more care on a sick lamb or a superfluous young pig than most of the neighbours' babies received.

So when one evening in May, Gray came in holding a bundle in his arms and poked it into her lap as she sat darning the holes in Tom's stockings (she was not good at needlework, but she managed, as she said, to 'goblify' the holes), he knew pretty well that it was into no unwilling arms that he gave the baby.

'And a mercy it was as the darning-needle didn't run right into the little angel,' Mrs Gray always said in recounting the story.

He had been down to the village to fetch some tobacco, for the Grays' cottage was right away from the village, up a lane leading on to the hillside, and there were no other cottages near. Tom was in bed, though it was not eight yet—but he was generally ready for bed when he had had his tea; and Bill was up on the hill, a favourite resort of his, and especially when it was growing dark and the great indigo sky spread over him, with the glory of the stars coming out.

'He never were like other lads,' his mother used to say with a mixture of pride and irritation; 'always mooning about by himself on them old hills.'

The cottage door stood open as it always did, and Mrs Gray sat there, plainly to be seen from the lane, with Tom's gray stocking and her eyes and the tallow candle as near together as possible. She did not hear a sound, though she was listening for Bill's return, and, even though Tom's snores penetrated the numerous crevices in the floor above, they were hardly enough to drown other sounds.

So there was no knowing when the bundle was laid just inside the cottage gate, not quite in the middle of the brick path, but on one side against the box edging, where a clump of daffodils nodded their graceful heads over the dark velvet polyanthus in the border. Gray nearly stepped upon the bundle, having large feet, and the way of walking which covers a good deal of ground to right and left, a way which plough-driving teaches.

Mrs Gray heard an exclamation.

And then Gray came in, and, as I have said, did his best to impale the bundle, baby and all, on the top of his wife's darning-needle.

CHAPTER II.

Mr Robins—Village Choirs—Edith—An Elopement—A Father's Sorrow—An Unhappy Pair—The Wanderer's Return—Father!—A Daughter's Entreater—No Favourable Answer—A Sleepless Pillow

The organist of Downside, Mr Robins, lived in a little house close to the church.

Mr Clifford the vicar was accounted very lucky by the neighbouring clergy for having such a man, and not being exposed to all the vagaries of a young schoolmaster, or, perhaps, still worse, schoolmistress, with all the latest musical fancies of the training colleges. Neither had he to grapple with the tyranny of the leading bass nor the conceit and touchiness that seems inseparable from the tenor voice, since Mr Robins kept a firm and sensible hand on the reins, and drove that generally unmanageable team, a village choir, with the greatest discretion.

But when Mr Clifford was complimented by his friends on the possession of such a treasure, he accepted their remarks a little doubtfully, being sometimes inclined to think that he would almost rather have had a less excellent choir and have had some slight voice in the matter himself.

Mr Robins imported a certain solemnity into the musical matters of Downside, which of course was very desirable as far as the church services were concerned; but when it came to penny-readings and village concerts, Mr Clifford and some of the parishioners were disposed to envy the pleasant ease of such festivities in other parishes, where, though the music was very inferior, the enjoyment of both performers and audience was far greater.

Mr Robins, for one thing, set his face steadily against comic songs; and Mr Clifford in his inmost heart had an ungratified ambition to sing a certain song, called 'The Three Little Pigs,' with which Mr Wilson in the next parish simply brought down the house on several occasions; though Mr Clifford felt he by no means did full justice to it, especially in the part where the old mother 'waddled about, saying "Umph! umph! umph!" while the little ones said "Wee! wee!"' To be sure Mr Wilson suffered for months after these performances from outbursts of grunting among his youthful parishioners at sight of him, and even at the Sunday-school one audacious boy had given vent on one occasion to an 'umph!' very true indeed to nature, but not conducive to good behaviour in his class. But Mr Clifford did not know the after effects of Mr Wilson's vocal success.

Likewise Mr Robins selected very simple music, and yet exacted an amount of practising unheard of at Bilton or Stokeley, where, after one or two attempts, they felt competent to face a crowded schoolroom, and yell or growl out such choruses as 'The Heavens are telling' or 'The Hallelujah Chorus,' with a lofty indifference to tune or time, and with their respective schoolmasters banging away at the accompaniment, within a bar or two of the singers, all feeling quite satisfied if they finished up altogether on the concluding chord or thereabouts, flushed and triumphant, with perspiration standing on their foreheads, and an expression of honest pride on their faces, as much as to say, 'There's for you. What do you think of that?'

If success is to be measured by applause, there is no doubt these performances were most successful, far more so than the accurately rendered 'Hardy Norseman' or 'Men of Harlech' at Downside, in which lights and shades, *pianos* and *fortes* were carefully observed, and any attempt on anyone's part, even the tenors, to distinguish themselves above the others was instantly suppressed. The result, from a musical point of view, was no doubt satisfactory; but the applause was of a very moderate character, and never accompanied by those vociferous 'angcores,' which are so truly gratifying to the soul of musical artistes.

Mr Robins was a middle-aged man, looking older than he really was, as his hair was quite white. He had some small independent means of his own, which he supplemented by his small salary as organist, and by giving a few music lessons in the neighbourhood. He had been in his earlier years a vicar-choral at one of the cathedrals, and had come to Downside twenty years ago, after the death of his wife, bringing with him his little girl, in whom he was entirely wrapt up.

He spoilt her so persistently, and his housekeeper, Mrs Sands, was so gentle and meek-spirited, that the effect on a naturally self-willed child can easily be imagined; and, as she grew up, she became more and more uncontrollable. She was a pretty, gypsy-looking girl, inheriting her sweet looks from her mother, and her voice and musical taste from her father. There was more than one young farmer in the neighbourhood who cast admiring glances towards the corner of the church near the organ, where the organist's pretty daughter sat, and slackened the pace of his horse as he passed the clipped yew-hedge by the church, to catch a glimpse of her in the bright little patch of garden, or to hear her clear sweet voice singing over her work.

But people said Mr Robins thought no one good enough for her, and though he himself had come of humble parentage, and in no way regarded himself, nor expected to be regarded as a gentleman, it was generally understood that no suitor except a gentleman would be acceptable for Edith.

And so it took every one by surprise, and no one more so than her father, when the girl took up with Martin Blake, the son of the blacksmith in the next village, who might be seen most days with a smutty face and leathern apron hammering away at the glowing red metal on the anvil. It would have been well for him if he had only been seen thus, with the marks of honest toil about him; but Martin Blake was too often to be seen at the 'Crown,' and often in a state that anyone who loved him would have grieved to see; and he was always to be found at any race meetings and steeplechases and fairs in the neighbourhood, and, report said, was by no means choice in his company.

To be sure he was good-looking and pleasant-mannered, and had a sort of rollicking, light-hearted way with him, which was very attractive; but still it seemed little short of infatuation on the part of Edith Robins to take up with a man whose character was so well known, and who was in every way her inferior in position and education.

No doubt Mr Robins was very injudicious in his treatment of her when he found out what was going on, and as this was the first time in her life that Edith's wishes had been crossed, it was not likely that she would yield without a struggle. The mere fact of opposition seemed to deepen what was at first merely an ordinary liking into an absorbing passion. It was perfectly useless to reason with her; she disbelieved all the stories to his discredit, which were abundant, and treated those who repeated them as prejudiced and ill-natured.

It was in vain that Mr Robins by turns entreated and commanded her to give him up, her father's distress or anger alike seemed indifferent to her; and when he forbade Martin to come near the place, and kept her as much as possible under his eye to prevent meetings between them, it only roused in her a more obstinate determination to have her own way in spite of him. She was missing one morning from the little bedroom which Mrs Sands loved to keep as dainty and pretty as a lady's, and from the garden where the roses and geraniums did such credit to her care, and from her place in the little church where her prayer-book still lay on the desk as she had left it the day before.

She had gone off with Martin Blake to London, without a word of sorrow or farewell to the father who had been so foolishly fond of her, or to the home where her happy petted childhood had passed. It nearly broke her father's heart; it made an old man of him and turned his hair white, and it seemed to freeze or petrify all his kindliness and human sympathy.

He was a proud, reserved man, and could not bear the pity that every one felt for him, or endure the well-meant but injudicious condolences, mixed with 'I told you so,' and 'I 've thought for a long time,' which the neighbours were so liberal with. Even Mr Clifford's attempts at consolation he could hardly bring himself to listen to courteously, and Jane Sands' tearful eyes and quivering voice irritated him beyond all endurance. If there had been anyone to whom he could have talked unrestrainedly and let out all the pent-up disappointment and wounded love and tortured pride that surged and boiled within him, he might have got through it better, or rather it might have raised him, as rightly borne troubles do, above his poor, little, pitiful self, and nearer to God; but this was just what he could not do.

He came nearest it sometimes in those long evenings of organ playing, of the length of which poor little Jack Davis, the blower, so bitterly complained, when the long sad notes wailed and sobbed through the little church like the voice of a weary, sick soul making its complaint. But even so he could not tell it all to God, though he had been given that power of expression in music, which must make it easier to those so gifted to cry unto the Lord.

But the music wailed itself into silence, and Jack in his corner by the bellows waited terror-struck at the 'unked' sounds and the darkening church, till he ventured at last to ask: 'Be I to blow, mister? I 'm kinder skeered like.'

So the organist's trouble turned him bitter and hard, and changed his love for his daughter into cold resentment; he would not have her name mentioned in his presence, and he refused to open a letter she sent him a few weeks after her marriage, and bid Jane Sands send it back if she knew the address of the person who sent it.

On her side, Edith was quite as obstinate and resentful. She had no idea of humbling herself and asking pardon. She thought she had quite a right to do as she liked, and she believed her father would be too unhappy without her to bear the separation long. She very soon found out the mistake she had made—indeed, even in the midst of her infatuation about Martin Blake, I think there lurked a certain distrust of him, and they had not been married many weeks—I might almost say days—before this distrust was more than realised.

His feelings towards her, too, had been mere flattered vanity at being preferred by such a superior sort of girl than any deeper feeling, and vanity is not a sufficiently lasting foundation for married happiness, especially when the cold winds of poverty blow on the edifice, and when the superior sort of girl has not been brought up to anything useful, and cannot cook the dinner, or iron a shirt, or keep the house tidy.

When his father, the old blacksmith at Bilton, died six months after they were married, Martin wished to come back and take up the work there, more especially as work was hard to get in London and living dear; but Edith would not hear of it, and opposed it so violently that she got her way, though Martin afterwards maintained that this decision was the ruin of him, occasionally dating his ruin six months earlier, from his wedding. Perhaps he was right, and he might have settled down steadily in the old home and among the old neighbours in spite of his fine-lady wife; but when he said so, Edith was quick to remember and cast up at him the stories which she had disbelieved and ignored before, to prove in their constant wranglings that place and neighbourhood had nothing to do with his idleness and unsteadiness. No one ever heard much of these five years in London, for Edith wrote no more after that letter was returned.

Those five years made little difference at Downside, except in Mr Robins' white hair and set lined face; the little house behind the yew-hedge looked just the same, and Jane Sands' kind, placid face was still as kind and placid. Some of the girls had left school and gone to service; some of the lads had developed into hobbledehoys and came to church with walking-sticks and well-oiled hair; one or two of the old folks had died; one or two more white-headed babies crawled about the cottage floors; but otherwise Downside was just the same as it had been five years before, when, one June morning, a self-willed girl had softly opened the door under the honeysuckle porch and stepped out into the dewy garden, where the birds were calling such a glad good-morning as she passed to join her lover in the lane.

But the flame of life burns quicker and fiercer in London than at Downside, for that same girl, coming back after only five years in

London, was so changed and aged and altered that—though, to be sure, she came in the dusk and was muffled up in a big shawl—no one recognised her, or thought for a moment of pretty, coquettish, well-dressed Edith Robins, when the weary, shabby-looking woman passed them by. She had lingered a minute or two by the churchyard gate, though tramps, for such her worn-out boots and muddy skirts proclaimed her, do not, as a rule, care for such music as sounded out from the church door, where Mr Robins was consoling himself for the irritation of choir-practice by ten minutes' playing. It was soon over, and Jack Davis, still blower, and not much taller than he was five years before, charged out in the rebound from the tension of long blowing, and nearly knocked over the woman standing by the churchyard gate in the shadow of the yew-tree, and made the baby she held in her arms give a feeble cry.

'Now then, out of the way!' he shouted in that unnecessarily loud voice boys assume after church, perhaps to try if their lungs are still capable of producing such a noise after enforced silence.

The woman made no answer, but after the boy had run off, went in and waited in the porch till the sound of turning keys announced that the organist was closing the organ and church for the night. But as his footsteps drew near on the stone pavement she started and trembled as if she had been afraid, and when he came out into the porch she shrank away into the shadow as if she wished to be unobserved. He might easily have passed her, for it was nearly dark from the yew-tree and the row of elms that shut out, the western sky, where the sunset was just dying away. His mind, too, was occupied with other things, and he was humming over the verse of a hymn the boys had been singing—'Far from my heavenly home.' There was no drilling into them the proper rendering of the last pathetic words—

> O guide me through the desert here,
> And bring me home at last.

He quite started when a hand was laid upon his arm, and a voice, changed indeed, and weak, but still the voice that in old days—not so very old either—was the one voice for him in all the world, said: 'Father!'

I think just for one minute his impulse was to take her in his arms and forget the ingratitude and desertion and deceit, like the father in the parable whose heart went out to the poor prodigal while he was yet a long way off; but the next moment the cold, bitter, resentful feelings quenched the gentler impulse, and he drew away his arm from her detaining hold, and passed on along the flagged path as if he were unconscious of her presence, and this on the very threshold of His house, who so pitifully forgives the debts of His servants, forasmuch as they have not to pay.

But he had not reached the churchyard gate before she was at his side again.

'Stop,' she said; 'you must hear me. It's not for my own sake, it's the child. It's a little girl; the others were boys, and I didn't mind so much; if they 'd grown up, they might have got on somehow—but there! they 're safe anyhow—both of them in one week,' wailed the mother's voice, protesting against her own words that she did not mind about them. 'But this is a girl, and not a bit like him. She 's like me, and you used to say I was like mother. She's like mother, I 'm sure she is. There, just look at her. It's so dark, but you can see even by this light that she's not like the Blakes.' She was fumbling to draw back the shawl from the baby's head with her disengaged hand, while with the other she still held a grip on his arm that was almost painful in its pressure; but he stood doggedly with his head turned away, and gave no sign of hearing what she said.

'He left me six months ago,' she went on, 'and I 've struggled along somehow. I don't want ever to see him again. They say he's gone to America, but I don't care. I don't mind starving myself, but it's the little girl—Oh! I 've not come to ask you to take me in, though it wouldn't be for long,' and a wretched, hollow cough that had interrupted her words once or twice before, broke in now as if to confirm what she said; 'if you'd just take the child. She's a dear little thing, and not old enough at two months to have learnt any harm, and Jane Sands would be good to her, I know she would, for the sake of old times. And I'll go away and never come near to trouble you again—I 'll promise it. Oh! just look at her! If it wasn't so dark you'd see she was like mother. Why, you can feel the likeness if you just put your hand on her little face; often in the night I 've felt it, and I never did with the boys. She's very good, and she's too little to fret after me, bless her!—and she 'll never know anything about me, and needn't even know she has a father, and he 's not ever likely to trouble himself about her.'

Her voice grew more and more pleading and entreating as she went on, for there was not the slightest response or movement in the still figure before her, less movement even than in the old yew-tree behind, whose smaller branches, black against the sky where the orange of the sunset was darkening into dull crimson, stirred a little in the evening air.

'Oh! you can't refuse to take her! See, I'll carry her as far as the door so that Jane can take her, and then I 'll go clear away and never come near her again. You 'll have her christened, won't you? I 've been thinking all the weary way what she should be called, and I thought, unless you had a fancy for any other name' (a little stifled sigh at the thought of how dear one name used to be to him), 'I should like her to be Zoe. Just when she was born, and I was thinking, thinking of you and home and everything, that song of yours kept ringing in my head, "Maid of Athens," and the last line of every verse beginning with Zoe. I can't remember the other words, but I know you said they meant "My life, I love you;" and Zoe was life, and I thought when I'm gone my little girl would live my life over again, my happy old life with you, and make up to you for all the trouble her mother's been to you.'

She stopped for want of breath and for the cough that shook her from head to foot, and at last he turned; but even in that dim light she could see his face plainly enough to know that there was no favourable answer coming from those hard set lips and from those cold steady eyes, and her hand dropped from his arm even before he spoke.

'You should have thought of this five years ago,' he said. 'I do not see that I am called upon to support Martin Blake's family. I must trouble you to let me pass.'

She fell back against the trunk of the yew-tree as if he had struck her, and the movement caused the baby to wake and cry, and the sound of its little wailing voice followed him as he walked down the path and out into the road, and he could hear it still when he reached his own garden gate, where through the open door the light shone out from the lamp that Jane Sands was just carrying into his room, where his supper was spread and his armchair and slippers awaited him.

In after days, remembering that evening, he fancied he had heard 'Father' once more mingling with the baby's cry; but he went in and shut the door and drew the bolt and went into the cheerful, pleasant room, leaving outside the night and the child's cry and the black shadow of the church and the yew-tree.

It was only the beginning of the annoyance, he told himself; he must expect a continued course of persecution, and he listened, while he made a pretence of eating his supper, for the steps outside and the knock at the door, which would surely renew the unwarrantable attempt to saddle him with the charge of the child. He listened too, as he sat after supper, holding up the newspaper in front of his unobservant eyes; and he listened most of the night as he tossed on his sleepless pillow—listened to the wind that had risen and moaned and sobbed round the house like a living thing in pain—listened to the pitiless rain that followed, pelting down on the ivy outside and on the tiles above his head, as if bent on finding its way in to the warm comfortable bed where he lay.

CHAPTER III.

Something on the Doorstep—Bill Gray—Is That a Cat?—She's Like Mother—A Baby's Shoe—Jane Restless

B

ut the annoyance for which Mr Robins had been preparing himself was not repeated; the persecution, if such had been intended, was not continued. As the days passed by he began to leave off listening and lying awake; he came out from his house or from the church without furtive glances of expectation to the right and left; he lost that constant feeling of apprehension and the necessity to nerve himself for resistance. He had never been one to gossip or concern himself with other people's matters, and Jane Sands had never brought the news of the place to amuse her master, as many in her place would have done; so now he had no way of knowing if his daughter's return had been known in the place, or what comments the neighbours passed on it.

He fancied that Jane looked a little more anxious than usual; but then her sister was lying ill at Stokeley, and she was often there with her, so that accounted for her anxiety. It accounted, too, for her being away one evening a fortnight later, when Mr Robins coming in in the dusk found something laid on his doorstep. His thoughts had been otherwise occupied, but the moment his eyes fell on the shepherd's-plaid shawl wrapping the bundle at his feet, he knew what it was, and recognised a renewed attempt to coerce him into doing what he had vowed he would not. He saw it all in a minute, and understood that now Jane Sands was in the plot against him, and she had devised this way of putting the child in his path because she was afraid to come to him openly and say what she wanted. Perhaps even now she was watching, expecting to see him fall into the trap they had set for him; but they should find they were very much mistaken.

His first resolution was to fetch the police constable and get him to take the child right off to the workhouse, but on second thoughts he altered his purpose. Such a step would set all the tongues in the place wagging, and, little as he cared for public opinion, it would not be pleasant for every one to be telling how he had sent his grandchild to the workhouse. Grandchild? pshaw! it was Martin Blake's brat.

The child was sleeping soundly, everything was quiet, the dusk was gathering thick and fast. Why should he not put the child outside some other cottage, and throw the responsibility of disposing of it on someone else, and be clear of it himself altogether? The idea shaped itself with lightning rapidity in his brain, and he passed quickly in review the different cottages in the place and their inmates, and in spite of his indifference to Martin Blake's brat, he selected one where he knew a kindly reception, at any rate for the night, would be given. He knew more about the Grays than of most of the village people. Bill was a favourite of his, and had been with him that afternoon after school to fetch a book Mr Robins had promised to lend him. He was a bright, intelligent boy, and had a sweet voice, and the organist found him a more apt pupil than any of the others, and had taken some pains with him, and when he was ill the winter before had been to see him, and so had come to know his mother, and her liking for anything young and weak and tender.

Their cottage was at some distance, to be sure, and Mr Robins had not had much to do with babies of late years, and was a little distrustful of his ability to carry one so far without rousing it and so proclaiming its presence, but there was a path across the fields but little frequented, by which he could convey the child without much risk of being met and observed.

And now the great thing to aim at was to carry out his plan as quickly as possible, before any one was aware of the child being at his house; and he gathered up the little warm bundle as gingerly as he knew how, and was on his way to the gate, when the sound of approaching steps along the road made him draw back and, unlocking the door, carry the child in. The steps stopped at the gate and turned in, and one of the choirmen came to the door.

There were little movements and soft grumblings inside the shawl in the organist's arms, and he turned quite cold with apprehension.

'Anyone at home?' sounded Millet's jovial voice at the open door. "Evening, Mr Robins—are you there? All in the dark, eh? I wanted a couple of words with you about that song.'

'I 'll come directly,' sounded the organist's voice, with a curious jogging effect in it, such as Millet was used to sometimes in his conversations with his wife at the children's bed-time. And then Millet heard him go up-stairs, and it was some minutes before he came down again, and then in such a queer absent condition that if it had been any other man in the parish than Mr Robins, whose sobriety was unimpeachable, Millet would have said that he had had a drop too much.

He did not ask him in or strike a light, but stood at the door answering quite at haphazard, and showing such indifference on the vital question of a certain song suiting Millet's voice, that that usually good-natured man was almost offended.

'Well, I 'll wish you good evening,' he said at last (it seemed to Robins that he had been hours at the door); 'perhaps you 'll just think it over and let me know. Hullo!—is that a cat you have up there? I thought I heard something squeal out just then.'

Mr Robins was not generally given to shaking hands—indeed, some of the choir thought he was too much stuck up to do so; but just then he seized Millet's hand and shook it quite boisterously, at the same time advancing with the apparent intention of accompanying him in a friendly manner to the gate, a movement which compelled Millet to back in the same direction, and cut short his farewell remarks, which frequently lasted for ten minutes or more. And all the way to the gate Robins was talking much quicker and louder than was his usual custom, and he ended by almost pushing Millet out at the gate, all the time expressing great pleasure at having seen him, and pressing him to come in again any evening he could spare the time, and have a pipe and a bit of supper with him—such unheard-of hospitality that Millet went home quite persuaded that the old man was, as he expressed it to his wife, 'going off his chump;' so that it was quite a relief to meet him two days later at the choir practice as formal and distant in his manners as ever.

Meanwhile Mr Robins had hastened back to his bedroom where the baby lay asleep on his bed; for it had been really Jane Sands' cat whose voice Millet heard, and not, as Mr Robins believed, the waking child's.

It was quite dark up there, and he could only feel the warm, little heap on his bed, but he struck a match to look at it. The shawl had fallen away, showing its little dark head and round sleeping face, with one little fist doubled up against its cheek and half-open mouth, and the other arm thrown back, the tiny hand lying with the little moist, creased palm turned up.

'She's like mother, I 'm sure she is.' He remembered the words and scanned the small sleeping face. Well, perhaps there was a likeness, the eyelashes and the gypsy tint of the complexion; but just then the match went out and the organist remembered there was no time to be wasted in trying to see likenesses in Martin Blake's brat. But just as he was lifting the baby cautiously from his bed, a sudden thought struck him. Zoe was to be her name; well, it should be so, though he had no concern in her name or anything else; so he groped about for pencil and paper, and wrote the name in big printing letters to disguise his hand and make it as distinct as possible, though even so, as we have seen already, the name caused considerable perplexity to the sponsors. And then he pinned the paper on to the shawl, and taking the child in his arms set out across the field path to the Grays' cottage.

There was a cold air, though it was a May night, but the child lay warm against him, and he remembered how its mother had said she could feel the likeness even in the dark, and he could not resist laying his cold finger on the warm little cheek under the shawl; and then, angry with himself for the throb that the touch sent to his heart, hastened his steps, and had soon reached the Grays' cottage and deposited his burden just inside the gate, where a few minutes after Gray found it. He could see Mrs Gray plainly as she sat at her work: a pleasant, motherly face; but he did not linger to look at it, but turned away and retraced his steps along the field path home. He found himself shivering as he went; the air seemed to have grown more chilly and penetrating without that warm burden against his heart, and the unaccustomed weight had made his arms tremble.

Somehow the house looked dull and uncomfortable, though Jane Sands had come in and lighted the lamp, and was laying his supper. Up-stairs there was a hollow on his bed where something had lain, and by the side of the bed he found a baby's woollen shoe, which might have betrayed him to Jane if she had gone up-stairs. But though he put it out of sight directly, he felt sure that the whole matter was no secret from Jane, and that she had been an accomplice in the trick that had been played on him, and he smiled to himself at the thought of how he had outwitted her, and of how puzzled she must be to know what had become of the baby.

He did his best to appear as tranquil and composed as usual, as if nothing had happened to disturb the ordinary current of his life, and he forced himself to make a few remarks on indifferent subjects when she came into the room.

She had evidently been crying, and was altogether in a nervous and upset condition. She forgot half the things he wanted at supper, and her hand trembled so that she nearly overturned the lamp. More than once she stopped and looked at him as if she were nerving herself to speak, and he knew quite well the question that was trembling on her lips. 'Where is the child? Master, where is the child?' But he would not help her in any way, and he quite ignored the agitation that was only too evident; and even when he went into the kitchen to fetch his pipe, and found her with her face buried in her arms on the kitchen table, shaking with irrepressible sobs, he retreated softly into the passage and called to her to bring the pipe, and when, after a long delay, she brought it in, he was apparently absorbed in his paper, and took no notice of her tear-stained face and quivering lips.

He heard her stirring far into the night, and once she went into the little room next his that used to be his daughter's, and which no one had used since she left, and in the silence of the night again he could hear heartbreaking sobs half-stifled.

'Poor soul! poor soul!' he said to himself. 'She's a good creature is Jane, and no doubt she's bitterly disappointed. I 'll make it up to her somehow. She's a faithful, good soul!'

He was restless and uncomfortable himself, and he told himself he had taken cold and was a bit feverish. It was feverish fancy, no doubt, that made him think the hollow where the child's light weight had rested was still perceptible, but this fancy outlasted the fever of that night and the cold that caused it, for there was hardly a night afterwards when Mr Robins did not detect its presence, even with all Jane Sands' thorough shaking of the feather-bed and careful spreading of sheets and blankets. If he dropped asleep for a minute that night the child was in his arms again, heavy as lead, weighing him down, down, down, into some unfathomable gulf, or he was feeling for it in the dark, and its face was cold as death; and more than once he woke with a start, feeling certain that a child's cry had sounded close to his bed.

CHAPTER IV.

Village Evidence—'Gray' on the Brain—Too Well He Knew—Mr Robins and the Baby—He Had Not Done Badly

There is certainly a penalty paid by people who keep entirely clear of gossip, though it is not by any means in proportion to the advantages they gain. The penalty is that when they particularly want to hear any piece of news, they are not likely to hear it naturally like other people, but must go out of their way to make inquiries and evince a curiosity which at once makes them remarkable.

Now every one in the village except Mr Robins heard of the baby found in the Grays' garden, and discussed how it came there, but it was only by overhearing a casual word here and there that the organist gathered even so much as that the Grays had resolved to keep the child, and were not going to send it to the workhouse. Even Bill Gray knew the organist's ways too well to trouble him with the story, though he was too full of it himself to give his usual attention at the next choir practice, and, at every available pause between chant and hymn, his head and that of the boy next him were close together in deep discourse.

It had occurred to Mr Robins' mind, in the waking moments of that restless night, that there might have been—nay, most probably was—some mark on the child's clothes which would lead to its identification, and, for the next few days, every glance in his direction, or, for the matter of that, in any other direction, was interpreted by him as having some covert allusion to this foundling grandchild of his; but the conversation of some men outside his yew-hedge, which he accidentally overheard one day, set his anxiety at rest.

From this he gathered that it was generally supposed to be a child belonging to a gypsy caravan that had passed through the village that day.

'And I says,' said one of the men with that slow, emphatic delivery in which the most ordinary sentiments are given forth as if they were wisdom unheard and undreamt of before; 'and I don't mind who hears me, as Gray did oughter set the perlice on to 'un to find the heartless jade as did 'un.'

'Ay, sure! so he did oughter; but he ain't on gumption, Gray ain't; never had neither, as have known him man and boy these fifty year.'

'My missus says,' went on the first speaker, 'as she seed a gypsy gal with just such a brat as this on her arm. She come round to parson's back door—my Liza's kitchen gal there and telled her mother. She were one of them dressed-up baggages with long earrings and a yeller handkercher round her head, a-telling fortunes; coming round the poor, silly gals with her long tongue and sly ways. She went in here, too.' Mr Robins guessed, though he could not see the jerk of the thumb in his direction. 'Mrs Sands told me so herself—the organist's listening was quickened to yet sharper attention—'she says she had quite a job to get rid of her, and thought she were after the spoons belike. But she says as she'd know the gal again anywheres, and my missus says she'd pretty near take her davy to the child, though as I says, one brat's pretty much like another—haw, haw! though the women don't think it.'

And the two men parted, laughing over this excellent joke.

It was most curious how that little out-of-the-way house of the Grays and its unremarkable inmates had suddenly become conspicuous; the very cottage was visible from all directions—from the churchyard gate, from the organist's garden, from various points along the Stokeley road; but perhaps this may have been because Mr Robins had never cared to identify one thatched roof from another hitherto. As for the Grays, they seemed to be everywhere; that man hoeing in the turnip-field was Gray, that boy at the head of the team in the big yellow wagon was Tom, and Bill seemed to be all over the place, whistling along the road or running round the corner, or waiting to change his book at the organist's gate. If Mr Clifford spoke to Mr Robins it was about something to do with the Grays, and even Mr Wilson of Stokeley stopped him in the road to ask if some people called Gray lived at Downside. It was most extraordinary how these people, so insignificant a week ago, were now brought into prominence.

Even before Mr Robins had overheard that conversation he had had a fidgety sort of wish to go up to the Grays' cottage, and now he made a pretext of asking for a book he had lent Bill, but went before the school came out, so that only Mrs Gray was at home as he opened the gate and went up the path.

It was a beautiful, sunny afternoon, and Mrs Gray was sitting outside the door, making, plain as she was, a pretty picture with the shadows of the young vine-leaves over the door dappling her print gown and apron and the baby's little dark head and pink pinafore, a garment that had once been Bill's, who had been of a more robust build than this baby, and moreover, had worn the pinafore at a more advanced age, so that the fit left a good deal to be desired, and the colour had suffered in constant visits to the wash-tub, and was not so bright as it had been originally.

But altogether, the faded pinafore and the vine-leaf shadows, and the love in the woman's face, made a harmonious whole, and the song she was singing, without a note of sweetness or tune in it, did not jar on the organist's ear, as you might have supposed, knowing his critical and refined taste.

'Good afternoon, Mrs Gray,' he said; 'I came for the book I lent your son the other day. Why, is this your baby?' he added with unnecessarily elaborate dissimulation. 'I did not know you had any so young.'

'Mine? Lor' bless you, no. Ain't you heard? Why, I thought it was all over the place. Gray, he found it in the garden just there where you be standing, a week ago come to-morrow. Ain't she a pretty dear, bless her! and takes such notice too, as is wonderful. Why, she's looking at you now as if she 'd aknown you all her life. Just look at her! if she ain't smiling at you, a little puss!'

'Where did she come from?'

'Well, sure, who 's to know? There was some gypsy folks through the place, and there 've been a lot of tramps about along of Milton Fair, and there was one of 'em, they say, a week or two ago with just such a baby as this 'un. My master he 've made a few inquirements; but there! for my part I don't care if we don't hear no more of her folks, and Gray's much of the same mind, having took a terrible fancy to the child. And it's plain as she ain't got no mother worth the name, as would leave her like that, and neglected too shameful. As there ain't no excuse, to my way of thinking, for a baby being dirty, let folks be as poor as they may.'

Somewhere deep down in Mr Robins's mind, unacknowledged to himself, there was a twinge of resentment at this reflection on the mother's treatment of the baby.

'She 's as sweet as a blossom now,' went on Mrs Gray, tossing the baby up, who laughed and crowed and stretched its arms. Yes, he could see the likeness, he was sure of it; and it brought back to his mind with sudden vividness a young mother's look of pride and love as she held up her little girl for the father's admiration. Mother and child had then been wonderfully alike, and in this baby he could trace a likeness to both.

Mrs Gray went maundering on, as her manner was, interspersing her narrative with baby nonsense and endearments, and Mr Robins forgot his errand, which was, after all, only a pretext, and stood half-listening, and more than half back in the old days of memory, and once he so far forgot himself as to snap his fingers at the child, and touch one of its warm, little hands, which immediately closed round his finger with a baby's soft, tenacious grasp, from which it required a certain gentle effort to escape.

'A pleasant, chatty sort of man the organist,' Mrs Gray said, having talked nearly all the time herself, with only a word or two from him now and then as reply; 'and not a bit of pride about him, let folks say what they like. Why, he stopped ever so long and had a deal to say; and there, Bill, you just run down with the book, as he went off after all without it.'

Mr Robins went home slowly across the fields in a curiously softened frame of mind. Perhaps it was the soft west wind, fragrant with sweet spring scents of cowslips and cherry blossom, or the full glad sunshine on all the varied green of tree and hedge, a thousand tints of that 'shower of greennesses' poured down so lavishly by the Giver of all good things; perhaps it was the larks springing up from the clover in such an ecstasy of song; or perhaps it was the clasp of a baby's hand on his finger. He noticed the spring beauty round him as he had not noticed such things for many a day, stooping to pick a big, tasselled, gold-freckled cowslip, and stopping to let a newly-fledged, awkward, young bird hop clumsily out of the way, with a sort of tenderness and consideration for young things unusual to him.

His mind was more at rest than it had been for the last three weeks. The baby's crowing laughter seemed to drive out of his memory the wailing cry and the hollow cough and the sad, beseeching voice saying 'Father,' and then the pitiless beating rain, which had been haunting him for the last three weeks. The sight of the baby, loved and cared for, had taken away a misgiving, which he had hardly been conscious of himself. After all, he had not done badly by the child. Mrs Gray was a kind motherly sort of body, and used to babies, which Jane Sands was not, and she would do well by the child, and he himself could see, without any one being the wiser, that the child did not want for anything, though he would not be held responsible in any way for it.

CHAPTER V.

Jane Hard at Work—Clothes for the Baby—Jane Returns—Jane Singing over her Work—Jane's Selfish Absorption—For a Poor Person's Child—The Organist in Church

There was one thing that puzzled Mr Robins extremely, and this was Jane Sands' behaviour. He was convinced that she had been a party to the trick that had been played off on him, and she was evidently full of some secret trouble and anxiety, for which he could only account by attributing it to her disappointment about the baby, and perhaps distrust of the care that would be taken of it by others.

Mr Robins often discovered her in tears, and she was constantly going out for hours at a time, having always hitherto been almost too much of a stay-at-home. He suspected that these lengthened absences meant visits to the Grays' cottage, and that baby-worship that women find so delightful; but he found out accidentally that she had never been near the cottage since the baby's arrival, and when he made an excuse of sending a book by her to Bill to get her to go there, she met the boy at the bottom of the lane, and did not go on to the cottage.

As to what he had overheard the men saying about the gypsy girl, he felt sure that Jane had only said this to put people on the wrong scent, though, certainly, deception of any sort was very unlike her. Once he found her sitting up late at night at work on some small frocks and pinafores, and he thought that at last the subject was coming to the surface, and especially as she coloured up and tried to hide the work when he came in.

'Busy?' he said. 'You seem very hard at work. Who are you working for?'

'A baby,' she stammered, 'a baby— —that my sister's taking care of.'

She was so red and confused that he felt sure she was saying what was not true, but he forgave her for the sake of the baby for whom he firmly believed the work was being done, and who, to be sure, when he saw it in Mrs Gray's arms, looked badly in want of clothes more fitted to its size than Bill's old pinafores.

He stood for a minute fingering the pink, spotted print of infantile simplicity of pattern, and listening to the quick click, click, of her needle as it flew in and out; but it was not till he had turned away and was half out of the kitchen, that she began a request that had been on the tip of her tongue all the time, but which she had not ventured to bring out while he stood at the table.

'I was going to ask—if you 'd no objection—seeing that they're no good to any one'— —

Now it was coming out, and he turned with an encouraging smile:

'Well, what is it?'

'There are some old baby-clothes put away in a drawer up-stairs. They 're rough dried, and I've kept an eye on them, and took them out now and then to see as the moth didn't get in them'— —

'Yes?'

'Well, sir—this baby that I'm working for is terrible short of clothes, and I thought I might take a few of them for her'— —

She did not look at him once as she spoke, or she might have been encouraged by the look on his face, which softened into a very benignant, kindly expression.

'To be sure! to be sure!' he said. 'I 've no objection to your taking some of them for the baby—at your sister's.' He spoke the last words with some meaning, and she looked quickly up at him and dropped her work as if tumultuous words were pressing to be spoken, but stopped them with an effort and went on with her work, only with heightened colour and trembling fingers.

She was not slow to avail herself of his permission, for that very night, before she went to bed, he heard her in the next room turning out the drawer where the old baby-clothes had been stored away ever since little Edith had discarded them for clothes of a larger size. And next morning she was up betimes, starching and ironing and goffering dainty little frills with such a look of love and satisfaction on her face, that he had not the heart to hint that she had availed herself somewhat liberally of his permission, and that less dainty care and crispness might do equally well for the baby, bundled up in Mrs Gray's kind but crumpling arms, to take the place of Bill's faded pinafore.

That afternoon he purposely took his way home over the hillside and down the lane by the Grays' cottage, with a conviction that he should see the baby tricked out in some of those frilled and tucked little garments over which Jane Sands had lavished so much time and attention that morning. But to his surprise he saw her in much the same costume as before, only the pinafore this time was washed-out lavender instead of pink, and, as she was in Bill's arms, and he, as the youngest of the family, being inexperienced in nursing, a more crumpled effect was produced than his mother had done. He could only conclude that Jane had not found time yet to take the things, or that Mrs Gray was reserving them for a more showy occasion.

But he found Jane just returning as he came up to his house, and she looked far more hot and dusty than the short walk up the lane to the Grays accounted for, but with a beaming look on her kind face that had not been there for many a day.

'Well,' he said, 'Jane, have you been to Stokeley?'

'Yes,' she said, 'and I took the things you were good enough to say the baby might have. They *were* pleased.'

She, too, spoke with a curious meaning in her voice and manner which somehow faded when she saw the want of response in his face. Indeed there was a very distinct feeling of disappointment and irritation in his feelings. For after all those clothes had actually gone to some other baby. Well! well! it is a selfish world after all, and each of us has his own interests which take him up and engross him. No doubt this little common child at Stokeley was all in all to Jane Sands, and she was glad enough of a chance to pick all the best out of those baby clothes up-stairs that he remembered his young wife preparing so lovingly for her baby and his. It gave him quite a pang to think of some little Sands or Jenkins adorned with these tucks he had seen run so carefully and frills sewn so daintily. He had evidently given Jane credit for a great deal more unselfishness and devotion to him and his than she really felt, for she had all the time been busy working and providing for her own people, when he had thought she was full of consideration for Edith's child. Pshaw! he had to pull himself together and take himself to task. For even in these few days he had grown to think of that little brown-faced, dark-eyed baby as his grandchild, instead of Martin Blake's brat. Insensibly and naturally, too, the child had brought back the memory of its mother, first as baby, then as sweet and winsome little child; then as bright, wilful, coaxing girl, and, lastly, unless he kept his thoughts well in check, there followed on these brighter memories the shadow of a white worn woman under the yew-tree in the churchyard, and of a voice that said 'Father.'

That uninteresting child at Stokeley apparently required a great supply of clothes, for Jane Sands was hard at work again that evening, and when he came in from the choir practice, he heard her singing over her work as she used to do in old days, and when he went in for his pipe, she looked up with a smile that seemed to expect a sympathetic response, and made no effort to conceal the work as she had done the day before.

He stood morosely by the fireplace for a minute, shaking the ashes out of his pipe.

'You're very much taken up with that baby,' he said crossly; and she looked up quickly, thinking that perhaps he had a hole in his stocking, or a button off his shirt to complain of, as a consequence of her being engrossed in other work. But he went on without looking at her, and apparently deeply absorbed in getting an obstinate bit of ash out of the pipe bowl.

'There's a child at Mrs Gray's they say is very short of clothes. That baby, you know'— —

'That baby that was found in the garden,' Jane said in such a curiously uninterested tone of voice that he could not resist glancing round at her; but she was just then engaged in that mysterious process of 'stroking the gathers,' which the intelligent feminine reader will understand requires a certain attention. If this indifference were assumed, Jane Sands was a much better actor and a more deceptive character than he had believed possible; if she were too entirely absorbed in her own people to give even a thought to her young mistress's baby, she was not the Jane Sands he thought he had known for the last twenty years. The only alternative was that she knew nothing about the baby having been left on his door-step, nor of the meeting with his daughter in the churchyard which had preceded it.

What followed convinced him that this was the case, though it also a little favoured the other hypothesis of her selfish absorption in her own people.

'Perhaps,' he said, 'you could look out some of those baby things up-stairs if there are any left.'

'What? I beg your pardon, sir. What did you say?'

'Those baby clothes up-stairs that you gave to your sister's baby.'

'Those!' she said, with a strange light of indignation in her eyes, more even than you would have expected in the most grasping and greedy person on a proposal that something should be snatched from her hungry maw and given to another. 'Those! Little Miss Edith's things! that her own mother made and that I 've kept so careful all these years in case Miss Edith's own should need them!'

You see she forgot in the excitement of the moment that these were the very things she had been giving away so freely to that common little child at Stokeley; but women are so inconsistent.

'Well?' he said, as her breath failed her in this unusual torrent of remonstrance. 'Why not?'

'For a little gypsy child! a foundling that nobody knows anything about! Don't do it, master, don't! I couldn't abear to see it. Here, let me get a bit of print and flannel and run together a few things for the child. I 'd rather do it a hundred times than that those things should be given away—and just now too!'

It was very plain to Mr Robins that she did not know; but all the same he was half inclined to point out that it was not a much more outrageous thing to bestow these cherished garments on a foundling than on her sister's baby; but she was evidently so unconscious of her inconsistency in the matter that he did not know how to suggest it to her.

'I 'm going into Stokeley to-morrow,' she went on, 'and if you liked I could get some print and make it a few frocks. I saw some very neat at fourpence three-farthings that would wash beautiful, and a good stout flannel at elevenpence. Oh! not like that,' she said as he laid a finger on some soft Saxony flannel with a pink edge which lay on the table. 'Something more serviceable for a poor person's child.'

Well, perhaps it was better that Jane should not know who the baby was of whom she spoke so contemptuously. A baby was none the better or healthier for being dressed up in frills and lace; and Mrs Gray was a thoroughly clean motherly woman, and would do well by the child.

All the same, when Jane came back from Stokeley next day and unfolded the parcel she had brought from the draper's there, he could not help feeling that that somewhat dingy lavender, though it might wash like a rag, was, to say the least, uninteresting, and the texture of the flannel, even to his undiscriminating eye, was a trifle rough and coarse for baby limbs.

He knew nothing (how should he?) of the cut and make of baby clothes, but somehow, these, under Jane's scissors and needle, did not take such attractive proportions as those she had prepared for the other baby; nor did the stitches appear so careful and minute, though Jane's worst enemy, if she had any, could not have accused her of putting bad work even into the hem of a duster, let alone a baby's frock. He also noticed that, industriously as she worked at the lavender print, her ardour was not sufficient to last beyond bedtime, and that, when the clock struck ten, her work was put away, without any apparent reluctance, even when, to all appearances, it was so near completion that anyone would have given the requisite ten minutes just from the mere desire of finishing.

That Sunday afternoon, when the curious name Zoe, sounding across the church in the strange clergyman's voice, startled the organist, who had not expected the christening to take place that day, one of the distracting thoughts which made him make so many mistakes in the music, was wondering what Jane Sands would think of the name, and whether it would rouse any suspicion in her mind and enlighten her a little as to who the baby at Mrs Gray's really was. The name was full of memories and associations to him; surely it must be also a little to Jane Sands.

But of all Sunday afternoons in the year, she had chosen this to go over to Stokeley church. Why, parson and clerk were hardly more regular in their attendance than Jane Sands as a rule; it was almost an unheard-of thing for her seat to be empty. But to-day it was so, and the row of little boys whom her gentle presence generally awed into tolerable behaviour, indulged unchecked in all the ingenious naughtiness that infant mind and body are capable of in church.

She came in rather late with his tea, apologising for having kept him waiting.

'It was christening Sunday,' she said, and then she looked at him rather wistfully.

Perhaps she has heard, he thought; perhaps the neighbours have told her the name, and she is beginning to guess.

'And the baby has been called'— — she hesitated and glanced timidly at him.

'Well?' he said encouragingly, 'what is the name?'

'Edith,' she answered, 'was one name.'

Pshaw! it was the baby at her sister's she was talking of all the time! He turned irritably away.

'He can't bear to hear the name, even now; or, perhaps, he's cross at being kept waiting for tea,' thought Jane Sands.

CHAPTER VI.

The Good Baby—Mr Robins Comes and Goes—A Secret Power—Mr Robins Happy—A Naughty Tiresome Gal!—The Gypsy Child

A

s spring glided into summer, and June's long, bright, hay-scented days passed by, followed by July, with its hot sun pouring down on the ripening wheat and shaven hayfields, and on the trees, which had settled down into the monotonous green of summer, the little, brown-faced baby at the Grays' throve and flourished, and entwined itself round the hearts of the kindly people in whose care Providence, by the hands of the organist, had placed it. It grew close to them like the branches of the Virginia creeper against a battered, ugly, old wall, putting out those dainty little hands and fingers that cling so close, not even the roughest wind or driving rain can tear them apart. Gray, coming in dirty and tired in the evening, after a long day's work in the hayfield or carting manure, was never too tired, nor for the matter of that too dirty, to take the baby, and let it dab its fat hands on his face, or claw at his grizzled whiskers or slobber open-mouthed kisses on his cheeks.

Tom, who had bought a blue tie, let Zoe scrabble at that vivid article, and pull the bit of southernwood out of his button-hole, and rumple his well-oiled locks out of all symmetry; while Bill expended boundless ingenuity and time in cutting whistles, and fashioning whirligigs, which were summarily disposed of directly they got into the baby's hands.

As for Mrs Gray, it is unnecessary to say that she was the most complete slave of all Zoe's abject subjects, and the neighbours all agreed that she was downright silly-like over that little, brown-faced brat as was no better—no, nor nothing to hold a candle to my Johnnie, or Dolly, or Bobby as the case might be.

An unprejudiced observer might have thought that Mrs Gray had some reason for her high opinion of Zoe, for she was certainly a very much prettier baby than the majority in Downside, who were generally of the dumpling type, with two currants for eyes. And she was also a very good baby—'And easy enough too for anyone to be good,' would be the comment of any listening Downside mother, 'when they always gets their own way!' which, however, is not so obvious a truth as regards babies under a year as it is of older people. Certainly to be put to bed awake and smiling at seven o'clock, and thereupon to go to sleep, and sleep soundly, till seven o'clock next morning, shows an amount of virtue in a baby which is unhappily rare, though captious readers may attribute it rather to good health and digestion, which may also be credited, perhaps, with much virtue in older people.

'And I do say,' Mrs Gray was never tired of repeating to anyone who had patience to listen, 'as nothing wouldn't upset that blessed little angel, as it makes me quite uneasy thinking as how she's too good to live, as is only natural to mortal babies to have the tantrums now and then, if it 's only from stomach-ache.'

The only person who seemed to sympathise in the Grays' admiration for the baby was the organist. It was really wonderful, Mrs Gray said, the fancy he had taken to the child—'Ay, and the child to him too, perking up and looking quite peart like, as soon as ever his step come along the path.' The wonder was mostly in the baby taking to him, in Mrs Gray's opinion, as there was nothing to be surprised at in anyone taking to the baby; but 'he, with no chick nor child of his own, and with that quiet kind of way with him as ain't general what children like; though don't never go for to tell me as Mr Robins is proud and stuck up, as I knows better.'

There was a sort of fascination about the child to the organist, and when he found that no one seemed to have the slightest suspicion as to who the baby really was, or why he should be interested in it, he gave way more and more to the inclination to go to the Grays' cottage, and watch the little thing, and trace the likeness that seemed every day to grow more and more strong to his dead wife and to her baby girl.

Perhaps anyone sharper and less simple than Mrs Gray might have grown suspicious of some other reason than pure, disinterested admiration for little Zoe, as the cause which brought the organist so often to her house; and perhaps, if the cottage had stood in the village street, it might have occasioned remarks among the neighbours; but he had always, of late years, been so reserved and solitary a man that no notice was taken of his comings and goings, and if his way took him frequently over the hillside and down the lane—why, it was a very nice walk, and there was nothing to be surprised at.

The only person who might have noticed where he went, and how long he sometimes lingered, was Jane Sands, and I cannot help thinking that in old days she would have done so; but then, as we have seen, she was not quite the same Jane Sands she used to be, or at any rate not quite what we used to fancy her, devoted above all things to her master and his interests, but much absorbed in her own matters, and in those Stokeley friends of hers. She had asked for a rise in her wages too, which Mr Robins assented to; but without that cordiality he might have done a few months before, and he strongly suspected that when quarter-day came, the wages went the same way as those baby clothes, for there was certainly no outlay on her own attire, which, though always scrupulously neat, seemed to him more plain and a shade more shabby than it used to be.

As the summer waxed and waned, the love for little Zoe grew and strengthened in the organist's heart. It seemed a kind of possession, as if a spell had been cast on him; in old times it might have been set down to witchcraft; and, indeed, it seemed something of the sort to himself, as if a power he could not resist compelled him to seek out the child—to think of it, to dream of it, to have it so constantly in his mind and thoughts, that from there it found its way into his heart. To us, who know his secret, it may be explained as the tie of blood, the drawing of a man, in spite of himself, towards his own kith and kin; blood is thicker than water, and the organist could not reject this baby grandchild from his natural feelings, though he might from his house. And beyond and above this explanation, we may account for it, as we may for most otherwise unaccountable things, as being the leading of a wise Providence working out a divine purpose.

Perhaps the punishment that was to come to the organist by the hands of little Zoe—those fat, dimpled, brown hands, that flourished about in the air so joyously when he whistled a tune to her—began from the very first, for it was impossible to think of the child without thinking of the mother, and to look at Zoe without seeing the likeness that his fond fancy made far plainer than it really was; and to think of the mother and to see her likeness was to remember that meeting in the churchyard, and the sad, pleading voice and hollow cough, and the cold denial he had given, and the beating rain and howling wind of that dreary night. He grew by degrees to excuse himself to himself, and to plead that he was taken unawares, and that, if she had not taken his answer as final, but had followed him to the house, he should certainly have relented.

And then he went a step further. I think it was one July day, when the baby had been more than usually gracious to him, and he had ventured, in Mrs Gray's absence, to lift her out of the cradle and carry her down the garden path, finding her a heavier weight than when he had first taken her to the Grays' cottage. She had clapped her hands at a great, velvet-bodied humble bee; she had nestled her curly head into his neck, and with the feeling of her soft breath on his cheek he had said to himself: 'If Edith were to come back now, I would forgive her for the baby's sake, for Zoe's sake.' He forgot that he had need to be forgiven too. 'She will come back,' he told himself, 'she will come back to see the child. She could not be content to hear nothing more of her baby and never to see her, in spite of what she said. And when she comes it shall be different, for Zoe's sake.'

He wondered if Jane Sands knew where Edith was, or ever heard from her. He sometimes fancied that she did, and yet, if she knew nothing of the baby, it was hardly likely that she had any correspondence with the mother. He was puzzled, and more than once he felt inclined to let her into the secret, or at least drop some hint that might lead to its discovery.

It pleased him to imagine her delight over Edith's child, her pride in, and devotion to it; she would never rest till she had it under her care, and ousted Mrs Gray from all share in little Zoe. And yet, whenever he had got so far in his inclination to tell Jane, some proof of her absorption in that baby at Stokeley, for whom he had a sort of jealous dislike, threw him back upon himself, and made him doubt her affection for her young mistress, and resolve to keep the secret to himself, at any rate for the present.

He came the nearest telling her one day in August, when, as he was watering his flowers in the evening, Mrs Gray passed the gate with that very little Zoe, who was so constantly in his thoughts.

She had a little white sun-bonnet on, which Jane Sands had actually bestowed upon her—rather grudgingly, it is true, and only because there was some defect about it which made it unworthy of the pampered child at Stokeley. Zoe saw the organist, or, at least,

Mrs Gray imagined that she did, for the cry she gave might equally well have been intended as a greeting to a pig down in the ditch.

'Well a-never, who 'd a' thought! she see you ever so far off, bless her! and give such a jump as pretty near took her out of my arms. Why there! Mr Robins don't want you, Miss Saucy, no one don't want such rubbige; a naughty, tiresome gal! as won't go to sleep, but keeps jumping and kicking and looking about till my arm's fit to drop with aching.'

Jane Sands was sitting at work just outside the kitchen door at the side of the house. He had seen her there a minute ago when he filled the watering-can at the pump, and a sudden impulse came into his mind to show her the child.

He did not quite decide what he should say, or what he should do, when the recognition, which he felt sure was unavoidable, followed the sight of the child; but he just yielded to the impulse, and took the child from Mrs Gray's arms and carried her round to the back-door. The recognition was even more instantaneous than he had expected. As he came round the corner of the house, with the little, white-bonneted girl in his arms, Jane sprang up with a cry of glad surprise and delight, such as swept away in a moment all his doubt of her loyalty to him and his, and all his remembrance of her absorption in that little common child at Stokeley. She made a step forward and then stood perfectly still, and the light and gladness faded out of her face, and her hands, that had been stretched out in delighted greeting, fell dull and lifeless to her sides.

He said nothing, but held the child towards her; it was only natural that she should doubt, being so unprepared, but a second glance would convince her.

'I thought,' she said, looking the baby over, with what in a less kind, gentle face, might have been quite a hard, critical manner, 'I thought for a minute'— —

'Well?'

'I was mistaken,' she said; 'of course I was mistaken.' And then she added to herself more than to him, 'It is not a bit like'— —

'Look again,' he said, 'look again; don't you see a likeness?'

'Likeness? Oh, I suppose it's the gypsy child up at Mrs Gray's, and you mean the likeness to the woman who came here that day she was left; but I don't remember enough of her to say. It's plain the child's a gypsy. What a swarthy skin, to be sure!'

Why, where were her eyes? To Mr Robins it was little Edith over again. He wondered that all the village did not see it and cry out on him.

But it was not likely that after this his confidence should go further, and just then the child began a little grumble, and he took her back hastily to Mrs Gray with a disappointed, crest-fallen feeling.

Jane Sands was conscious that her reception of the baby had not been satisfactory, and she tried to make amends by little complimentary remarks, which annoyed him more than her indifference.

'A fine, strong child, and does Mrs Gray great credit.'

'It's a nice bright little thing, and I daresay will improve as it grows older.'

She could not imagine why the organist grunted in such a surly way in reply to these remarks, for what on earth could it matter to him what anyone thought of a foundling, gypsy child?

CHAPTER VII.

Gray Taken to the Hospital—Bill and the Baby—Mrs Gray Home Again—Edith, Come Home!

It was near the end of September that John Gray broke his leg. They were thrashing out a wheat-rick at Farmer Benson's, and somehow he tumbled from the top of the rick, and fell with his leg bent under him, and found that he could not stand when he tried to struggle up to his feet.

They ran to tell 'his missus,' who came straight off from the wash-tub, with the soapsuds still about her skinny red elbows, catching up Zoe from the cradle as she passed, at sight of whom Gray, in spite of the pain and the deadly faintness that was dimming his eyes and clutching his breath, made an effort to chirrup and snap his fingers at the little one.

'It's his innerds as is hurted,' explained one of the bystanders, with that wonderful openness and way of making the worst of everything that is found in that class.

'The spine of his back most like,' said another, 'like poor Johnson, over to Stokeley, as never walked another step arter his fall.'

'Ay, he do look mortal bad! 'Tis a terrible bad job!'

'Cut off like a flower!' sighed one of the women. 'There, bear up, my dear,' to Mrs Gray, with whom she had not been on speaking terms for some weeks, owing to a few words about her cat's thieving propensities, 'Dontee take on! I knows well enough what you feels, as is only three weeks since father was took with his fit.'

'Don't be skeered, old gal,' sounded Gray's voice, odd and unnatural to the ears of the hearers, and far away and independent to himself, 'I ain't so bad as that comes to'— —

And then mercifully he became unconscious, for to go six miles with a broken leg in a cart without springs on the way to the hospital is not a joke, and the neighbours' kindly attempts to bring him round were happily unsuccessful. The worst part of that drive fell to the share of his wife, who sat holding his head on her lap as they jolted along, trying to keep the jars and bumps from jerking his leg, though all the time she firmly believed he was dead, and was already, in her dulled mind, making pitiful little arrangements about mourning and the funeral, and contemplating, with dreary equanimity, a widowed existence with three-and-sixpence a week for her and Tom and Bill and Zoe to live upon. She never left Zoe out of the calculation, even when it became most difficult to adjust the number of mouths to be fed with the amount of food to be put into them, and over this dark future fell the darker shadow of the workhouse, which closes the vista of life to most of the poor. No wonder they live entirely in the present, and shut their eyes persistently to the future!

There was not much going back into the past when she was a girl and the 'master' a lad, and they went courting of a Sunday afternoon along the green lanes. Life had been too matter-of-fact and full of hard work to leave much sentiment even in memory.

Mr Robins heard of the accident in the evening, and went up to the cottage, where he found Bill taking care of Zoe, who was having a fine time of it, having soon discovered that she had only to cry for anything that evening to get it, and that it was an occasion for displaying a will of her own in the matter of going to bed, and being preternaturally wide awake and inclined for a game, when on other nights she was quite content to be laid down in the wooden cradle, which was rapidly becoming too small for her increasing size.

Poor Bill had been at school when the accident happened, and, of course, the neighbours had made the very worst of the matter, so the poor boy hardly knew what part of his father had not been crushed or injured, or if he had been killed on the spot, or had been taken barely alive to the hospital. The baby had been pushed into his arms, so that he could not go up to the farm, nor find Tom to learn the rights of the matter; so that, when Mr Robins came into the cottage, he found both Bill and the baby crying together, the fire out, and the kettle upset into the fender.

'Give me the child,' the organist said. And Bill obeyed, as he did at the choir practice when he was told to pass a hymn-book, and too miserable to wonder much at this new aspect of his master, and at seeing him take the baby as if he knew all about it, and sit down in father's arm-chair.

'See if you can't make the fire burn up,' he went on; 'the child's cold.'

Zoe seemed well content with her new nurse, and left off crying, and sat blinking gravely at the fire, which Bill, much relieved at having something definite to do, soon roused up to a sparkling, crackling blaze with some dry sticks; while Mr Robins warmed her small, pink feet.

Bill would certainly have been surprised if he could have seen what was passing in the organist's mind, a proposal ripening into a firm resolve that he would take the child home that very night and tell Jane who she was. Let the village talk as it might, he did not mind; let them say what they pleased.

He knew enough of village reports to guess that Gray was not as badly hurt as every one declared; but still, even a trifling accident meant, at any rate, a week or two of very short commons at the cottage, perhaps less milk for the baby, or economy over fuel, and the September days were growing cold and raw, and there had been more than one frost in the mornings, and the baby's little toes were cold to his warm hand. Mrs Gray, too, would be occupied and taken up with her husband, and little Zoe would be pushed about from one to another, and he had heard that there was scarlatina about, and the relieving officer had been telling him that very morning how careless the people were about infection.

The cottage looked quite different in the blazing firelight, and Bill, encouraged by the organist's presence, tidied up the place, where the washtub stood just as Mrs Gray had left it; and he set the kettle on to boil, so that when Mrs Gray and Tom came in it presented quite a comfortable appearance.

Mrs Gray came in tired and tearful, but decidedly hopeful, having left Gray comfortably in bed with his leg set, and having received reassuring opinions from nurse and doctor: and the first alarm and apprehension being removed, there was a certain feeling of importance in her position as wife of the injured man, and excitement at a visit to the country town, both ways in a cart, which does not happen often in a life-time.

The baby, thanks to the warmth and Mr Robins's nursing, had fallen asleep in his arms. Mrs Gray was so much confused and bewildered by the events of the day, that she would hardly have been surprised to see the Queen with the crown on her head sitting there in the master's arm-chair, quite at home like, and holding the baby on one arm and the sceptre on the other; and Tom was of too phlegmatic a disposition to be surprised at anything. So they made no remark, and Mr Robins laid the baby, still asleep, in Bill's arms, and went away.

Such a beautiful, quiet September night, with great, soft stars overhead, and the scent of fallen leaves in the air; the path beneath his feet was soft with them, and as he passed under the elms which by daylight were a blaze of sunny gold, some leaves dropped gently on his head.

'To-morrow,' he said, 'I will bring little Zoe home, and I will let her mother—I will let Edith know that the child is with me, and that if she likes'—— It needed but a word, he felt sure, to bring the mother to the baby, the daughter to her father.

He stood for a moment by the church-yard gate, close to the spot where that bitter, cruel parting had been, and fancied what the meeting would be. After all, what was his feeling for little Zoe, and his imagination of what his little grandchild would be to him in the future, to the delight of having Edith's arms round his neck and holding her to his heart once more?

'Edith,' he whispered softly, as he turned away; 'Edith, come home!'

'I wonder,' he said to Jane Sands that night; 'I wonder if you could find out an address for me?'

She was folding up the tablecloth, and she stopped with a puzzled look.

'An address? Whose?'

'Well,' he said, without looking at her, 'I fancy there are still some of the Blakes, (the word came out with a certain effort) 'living at Bilton, and perhaps you could find out from them the address I want; or, perhaps,' he added quickly, for she understood now, and eager words were on her lips, 'perhaps you know. There! never mind now; if you know, you can tell me to-morrow.'

CHAPTER VIII.

Preparation—The Room Furnished—Mrs Gray at Work—The Baby Gone—The Gypsy Mother—The Gypsy's Story—A Foolish Fancy—Something Has Happened—The Real Baby

Morning very often brings other counsels, but this was not the case with Mr Robins, for when he got up next day he was more than ever resolved to carry out his intention of bringing little Zoe home, and letting her mother know that a welcome awaited her in her old home.

He had not slept very much during the night, for his mind had been too full of the change that was coming in his life, and of the difference that the presence of Edith and little Zoe would make in the dull, old house. Sad and worn and altered, was she! Ah! that would soon pass away with kindness and care and happiness, and the cough that had sounded so hollow and ominous should be nursed away, and Edith should be a girl again, a girl as she ought to be yet by right of her years; and those five years of suffering and estrangement should be altogether forgotten as if they had never been.

He went into the bedroom next his, that had been Edith's—that was to be Edith's again—and, looking round it, noticed with satisfaction that Jane had kept it just as it had been in the old days; and he pushed the bed a little to one side to make room for a cot to stand beside it, a cot which he remembered in the night as having stood for years in the lumber-room up in the roof, and which he now with much difficulty dragged out from behind some heavy boxes, and fitted together, wishing there had been time to give it a coat of paint, and yet glad, with a tremulous sort of gladness, that there was not, seeing that it would be wanted that very night.

And just then Jane Sands came up to call him to breakfast, and stood looking from the cot to her master's dusty coat, with such a look of delighted comprehension on her face, that the organist felt that no words were needed to prepare her for what was going to happen.

'I thought,' he said, 'it had better be brought down.'

'Where shall it go?' she asked.

'In Miss— —in the room next mine,' he said, 'and it will want a good airing.'

'Shall I make up the bed too?' she asked.

'Yes, you may as well.'

'Oh, master,' she said, the tears shaking in her voice and shining in her eyes; 'will they be wanted soon? Will they, maybe, be wanted to-night?'

His own voice felt suspiciously shaky; his own eyes could not see the old cot, nor Jane's beaming face quite plainly, so he only gave a gruff assent and turned away.

'What a good, kind creature she is!' he thought. 'What a welcome she will give Edith and Edith's little Zoe!'

During the morning he heard her up in the room sweeping and scrubbing, as if for these five years it had been left a prey to dust and dirt; and when he went out after dinner to give a lesson at Bil ton, she was still at it with an energy worthy of a woman, half her age.

That stupid little girl at Bilton, who generally found her music-lesson such an intolerable weariness to the flesh, and was conscious that it was no less so to her teacher, found the half-hour to-day quite pleasant. Mr Robins had never been so kind and cheerful, quite amusing, laughing at her mistakes, and allowing her to play just the things she knew best, and to get up in the middle of the lesson to go to the window and see a long procession of gypsy vans going by to Smithurst fair.

It was such a very beautiful day; perhaps it was this that produced such a good effect on the organist's temper. There had been a frost that morning, but it was not enough to strip the trees, but only to turn the elms a richer gold, and the beeches a warmer red, and the oaks a ruddier brown; while in the hedges the purple dogwood, and hawthorn, and bramble leaves made a wonderful variety of rich tints in the full bright sunshine, which set the birds twittering with a momentary delusion that it might be spring.

He did not come back over the hill, and past the Grays' cottage, for he was going to fetch the child that evening; but he came home by the road, meeting many more of those gypsy vans which had distracted his pupil's attention, and looking with kindliness on the swarthy men and bronze dark-eyed women, for the sake of little Zoe, who had been so often called the gypsy baby.

When he reached home he found the room prepared with all the care Jane Sands could lavish. He had thought when he went in that morning that it was just as Edith had left it, and all in the most perfect order; but now the room was a bower of daintiness and cleanliness, and all Edith's old treasures had been set out in the very order she used to arrange them—why! even her brush and comb were laid ready on the dressing-table, and a pair of slippers by the bedside, and a small bunch of autumn anemones and Czar violets was placed in a little glass beside her books. He smiled, but with tears in his eyes, as he saw all these loving preparations.

'Edith can hardly be here to-night,' he said to himself, 'but Zoe will.' And he smoothed the pillow of the cot close to the bedside, and drew the curtain more closely over its head.

He found his tea set ready for him when he came down, but Jane Sands had gone out, and he was rather glad of it, as she had watched him that morning with an eager expectant eye, and he did not know what to say to her. It would be easier when he brought the baby and actually put it into her arms.

The sun had set when he had finished tea, a blaze of splendour settling down into dull purple and dead orange, leaving a stripe of pale-green sky over the horizon, flecked with a few soft brown clouds tinged with red.

But envious night hastened to cover up and deaden the colours of the sky, and the almost equally gorgeous tints of tree and hedge; and, by the time Mr Robins reached the Grays' cottage, darkness had settled down as deep as on that evening four months ago, when he carried the baby and left it there.

Now, as then, the cottage door was open, and Mrs Gray sat at work with the candle close to her elbow, every now and then giving a long sniff or a sigh, that made the tallow candle flicker and tremble. He had almost forgotten her husband's accident in his absorption in the baby; but these sniffs recalled it to his mind, and he thought he would give them a helping hand while Gray was in the hospital.

'She has been kind to my little Zoe,' he thought, 'and I will not forget it in a hurry. She shall come and see the child whenever she likes; and Edith will be good to her, for she has been like a mother to the baby all these months.'

Close by where Mrs Gray sat he could see the foot of the old cradle and the rocker within reach of the woman's foot; but Zoe must be asleep, for there was no rocking necessary, and Mrs Gray did not turn from her work to look at the child, though she stopped from time to time to wipe her eyes on her apron.

'She is taken up with her husband,' he said to himself; 'it is as well that I am going to take the child away, as she will have no thought to give her now.'

And then he went into the cottage, with a tap on the open door to announce his presence.

'Good evening, Mrs Gray,' he said in a subdued voice, so as not to wake the baby. But he might have spared himself this precaution, for the next glance showed him that the cradle was empty.

'Bless you, Mr Robins,' the woman said, 'you give me quite a start, coming in so quiet like. But, there! I 'm all of a tremble, the leastest thing do terrify me. You might knock me down with a feather. First one thing and then another! The master yesterday and the baby today!'

'What!' he said, so sharp and sudden, that it stopped the flow of words for a moment. 'What do you mean! Is the baby in bed upstairs? What's the matter? It's not the scarlatina? Not'— —

'Bless you!' she said, 'why I thought you'd a-knowed. It ain't the scarlatina; the baby was as well and bonnie as ever when she went. She 've agone! her mother come and fetch her this very day, and took her right off. Ay! but she were pleased to see how the little thing had got on, and she said as she 'd never forget my kindness, and how she'd bring her to see me whenever she come this way.

But, there! I do miss her terrible. Why, it's 'most worse than the master himself.'

The organist hardly listened to what she was saying after the fact of the mother having come and fetched her away. Edith had come for her baby! How had she known? Why had she done it to-day? Could Jane have let her know? And had she come so quickly to take the child herself to her old home? His first impulse was to turn and hasten home; perhaps Edith and Zoe were there already, and would find him absent. But he could not go without a word to Mrs Gray, who was wiping her eyes in her apron and unconsciously rocking the empty cradle.

'You will often see her,' he said consolingly; 'she will not be very far away.'

'Oh, I don't know about that; them gypsies go all over the place, up and down the country, and they don't always come back for the fairs; though she says as they don't often miss Smithurst.'

'Gypsies?' he said puzzled.

'Ay, the mother 's a gypsy sure enough, and I've said it all along, and the child's the very image of her; there wasn't no doubt, when one saw the two together, as they was mother and child.'

'Are you sure she was a gypsy?' He had often said in fun that Edith was a regular little gypsy, but he would never have thought that any one could really mistake her for one; and besides, Mrs Gray must have known Edith well enough at any rate by sight in the old days; and changed as she was, it was not beyond all recognition.

'Oh, there wasn't no mistaking, and the van as she belonged to waited just outside the village, for I went down along with her and seed it, painted yeller with red wheels. I knowed Zoe was gypsy born, for she'd one of them charms round her neck as I didn't meddle with, for they do say as there's a deal of power in them things, and that gypsies can't be drownded or ketch fevers and things as long as they keeps 'em.'

Mr Robins sat down in the chair opposite Mrs Gray; an odd, cold sort of apprehension was stealing over him, and the pleasant dream of home and Edith and Zoe, in which he had been living through the day, was fading away with every word the woman said.

'The funny part of it were that she vowed and declared as she put the child at your door, and never came this way at all; leastways, from what she said it must abeen your house, for she said it was hard by the church and had a thick hedge, and that there was a kind sorter body as she see there in the morning, as must abeen Mrs Sands, and nobody else from her account. She said she was in a heap of trouble just then, her husband ill and a deal more, and she was pretty nigh at her wits' end, and that, without thinking twice what she were about, she wropt the baby up and laid it close agin the door of the house where she'd seen the kind-looking body. She would have it as it was there, say what I would; but, maybe, poor soul, she were mazed, and hardly knew where she were.

'She went to your house to-day, and Mrs Sands were quite put out with her, being busy too, and expecting company, and thought it were just her impidence; but there! I knows what trouble is, and how it just mazes a body, for I could no more tell where I went nor what I did yesterday than that table there. And another queer thing is as she didn't know nothing about the name, and neither she nor her husband can't read or write noways, so she couldn't have wrote it down, and she 'd never heard tell of such a name as Zoe, and didn't like it neither. She'd always ameant it to be Rachel, as had been her mother's name before her, and her grandmother's too.'

'Are you quite certain she was the mother?'

'Certain? Why, you 'd only to see the two together to be sure of it. I'd not have let her go, not were it ever so, if it hadn't been as clear as daylight; and just now too, when I seems to want her for a bit of comfort.' And here Mrs Gray relapsed into her apron.

Mr Robins sat for a minute looking at her in silence, and then got up, and without a word went out into the dark night, mechanically taking the way to his house, and then turning on to the high-road to Smithurst, tramping along through the mud and dead leaves with a dull, heavy persistence.

Anything was better than going back to the empty silence of his house and Jane Sands' expectant face, and the pretty, white-curtained room with the cot all ready for little Zoe, who was already miles away along that dark road before him, sleeping, perhaps, in some dirty gypsy van put up on some bit of waste land by the roadside, or, perhaps, surrounded by the noise and glare of the fair with its shows and roundabouts. His little Zoe! he could not possibly have been so utterly deceived all through; the baby who had lain on his bed, whose little face he had felt as he carried her up to the Grays' cottage in the dark, whom he had seen day after day, and never failed to notice the likeness, growing stronger with the child's growth. Was it all a delusion? all the foolish fancy of a fond, old man? He tried hard to believe that it was impossible that he could have been so deceived, and yet from the very first he felt that it was so, and that the love that had been growing in his heart all these months had been lavished on a gypsy baby whose face most likely he should never see again.

And all his plans for the future, his dreams of reparation, of tender reconciliation with Edith, and of happy, peaceful days that would obliterate the memory of past trouble and alienation, they had all vanished with the gypsy baby; life was as empty as the cradle by Mrs Gray's side.

Where was he to find his daughter? Where had she wandered that night when the pitiless rain fell and the sullen wind moaned? Was that the last he should ever see of her, with the white, wan, pleading face under the yew-tree? And would that despairing voice, saying 'Father!' haunt his ears till his dying day? And would the wailing cry that followed him as he went to his house that night be the only thing he should ever know of his grandchild, the real little Zoe whom he had rejected?

He was several miles away along the Smithurst road when he first realised what he was doing, brought to the consciousness, perhaps, by the fact of being weary and footsore and wet through from a fine rain that had begun falling soon after he left the village. It must be getting late too; many of the cottages he passed showed no light from the windows, the inmates most likely being in bed.

Painfully and wearily he toiled back to Downside; he seemed to have no spirit left to contend against even such trifling things as mud and inequalities in the road, and when a bramble straying from the hedge caught his coat and tore it, he could almost have cried in feeble vexation of spirit. Downside street was all dark and quiet, but from the organist's house a light shone out from the open door and down the garden path, making a patch of light on the wet road.

Some one stood peering out into the darkness, and, at the sound of his dragging, stumbling footsteps, Jane Sands ran down to the gate. The long waiting had made her anxious, for she was breathless and trembling with excitement.

'Where have you been?' she said; 'we got so frightened. Why are you so late? Oh, dearie me!' as she caught sight of his face. 'You 're ill! Something has happened! There, come in, doee, now; you look fit to drop!'

He pushed by her almost roughly into the house, and dropped down wearily into the arm-chair. He was too worn out and exhausted to notice anything, even the warmth and comfort of the bright fire and the supper ready on the table. He tossed his soaked hat on the ground, and leaning his elbows on his knees and his head on his hands, sat bowed down with the feeling of utter wretchedness.

Day after day, night after night, till his life's end, plenty and comfort and neatness and respectability and warmth in dull monotony; while outside somewhere in the cold and rain, in poverty and want and wretchedness, wandered Edith with the wailing baby in her arms.

'You can go to bed,' he said to Jane Sands; 'I don't want any supper.'

She drew back and went softly out of the room, but some one else was standing there, looking down at the bowed white head with eyes fuller even of pity and tears than Jane's had been; and then she, too, left the room, and with a raised finger to Jane, who was waiting in the passage, she went up-stairs and, as if the way were well known to her, to the little room which had been got ready so uselessly for the organist's daughter.

There, sheltered by the bed-curtain, was the cot where Zoe was to have lain, and there, wonderful to relate, a child's dark head might be seen, deep in the soft pillow, deeper in soft sleep.

And then this strangely presuming intruder in the organist's house softly took up the sleeping child, and wrapping a shawl round it, carried it, still sleeping, downstairs, the dark lashes resting on the round cheek flushed with sleep and of a fairer tint than gypsy Zoe's, and the rosy mouth half-open.

The organist still sat with his head in his hands, and did not stir as she entered, not even when she came and knelt down on the hearth in front of him.

Jane Sands was unusually tiresome to-night, he thought; why could she not leave him alone?

And then against his cold hands clasped over his face was laid something soft and warm and tender, surely a little child's hand! and a voice (a voice he had never thought to hear again till maybe it sounded as his accuser before the throne of grace) said: 'Father, for Zoe's sake.'

THE END.

Edinburgh;
Printed by W & R. Chambers, Limited.

FOR YOUNGER BOYS AND GIRLS

1s. net.-

LITTLE MARY . . . . L. T. Meade. SQUIRE'S LITTLE GIRL . . . . L. T. Meade. THE GREEN CASKET . . . . Mrs Molesworth. BEWITCHED LAMP . . . . Mrs Molesworth. THEIR HAPPIEST XMAS . . . . Edna Lyall. LASSIE . . . . By the Author of *Laddie*. BABY JOHN . . . . By the Author of *Laddie*. ZOE . . . . By the Author of *Laddie*. WILFRID CLIFFORD . . . . Edith C. Kenyon. ERNEST'S GOLDEN THREAD . . . . Edith C. Kenyon. THE LITTLE KNIGHT . . . . Edith C. Kenyon. A FAIRY GRANDMOTHER . . . . L. E. Tiddeman. HUMBLE HEROINE . . . . L. E. Tiddeman. STEADFAST GABRIEL . . . . Mary Howitt. UNCLE SAM'S MONEY-BOX . . . . Mrs S. C. Hall. SWAN'S EGG . . . . Mrs S. C. Hall. GRAMDMAMA'S POCKETS . . . . Mrs S. C. Hall. WONDERFUL STORIES . . . . Hans C. Andersen.

W. & R. CHAMBERS, LIMITED, LONDON AND EDINBURGH.

Printed in Great Britain.
W. & R. CHAMBERS, LTD., LONDON and EDINBURGH.